P9-ELV-177

Big Dog and Little Dog
Getting in Trouble

Dav Pilkey

Houghton Mifflin Harcourt
Boston New York

Copyright © 1997 by Dav Pilkey

Activities © 2015 by Houghton Mifflin Harcourt Publishing Company

For information about permission to reproduce selections from this book,

write to Permissions, Houghton Mifflin Harcourt Publishing Company,

215 Park Avenue South, New York, New York 10003.

Green Light Readers ® and its logo are trademarks of HMH Publishers LLC,

registered in the United States and other countries.

www.hmhco.com

Library of Congress Cataloging-in-Publication Data is on file.

ISBN: 978-0-544-53096-6 paper-over-board

ISBN: 978-0-544-53095-9 paperback

Manufactured in China

SCP 10 9 8 7 6 5 4 3 2 1

4500535521

Ages	Grades	Guided Reading Level	Reading Recovery Level	Lexile® Level
4–6	K	D	5–6	210L

To Kevin Alan Libertowski

Big Dog wants to play.

Little Dog wants to play, too.

But there is nothing to play with.

What will they play with?

Big Dog and Little Dog are playing.

They are playing with the couch.

Big Dog and Little Dog
are having fun.

Big Dog and Little Dog
are being bad.

Big Dog is making a mess.

Little Dog is making a mess.

Uh-oh.

Big Dog is in trouble.

Little Dog is in trouble, too.

Big Dog and Little Dog are sorry.

They will be good from now on.

❀ Spot the Differences ❀

There are eight differences between the
top picture and the bottom picture.
Can you find them all?

❧ Word Scramble ❧

These words from the story got mixed up!
Can you unscramble them and point to
the correct words in the Word Box?
Try writing a new story with these words!

Word Box

AYPL	FUN
UCOCH	LITTLE
NFU	PLAY
DAB	COUCH
IGB	GOOD
LETLIT	BAD
DOGO	BIG

Dog-Libs

Learning Nouns and Verbs

Ask a friend to make a list of
six nouns and three verbs.
Use the words to complete the story.
How silly is your new story?

Noun - a person, place, or thing
Verb - an action

Dogs are very playful. They will (verb) with a (noun) , a (noun) , or a (noun) . Sometimes, dogs will be very bad and play with a (noun) . When they do that, they make a big (noun) . When dogs (verb) , they should not (verb) with a (noun) !

 Fill-in-the-Blank

Choose the missing word from the Word Box to complete these sentences!

Word Box

fun
mess
play
trouble
couch
bad

Big Dog wants to _____ .

Big Dog and Little Dog are playing with the _____ .

Big Dog and Little Dog are having _____ .

Big Dog and Little Dog are being .

Big Dog and Little Dog are making a .

Big Dog is in big .